Dear Parent:

Buckle up! You are about to join your child on a very exciting journey. The destination? Independent reading!

Road to Reading will help you and your child get there. The program offers books at five levels, or Miles, that accompany children from their first attempts at reading to successfully reading on their own. Each Mile is paved with engaging stories and delightful artwork.

Getting Started
For children who know the alphabet and are eager to begin reading
• easy words • fun rhythms • big type • picture clues

Reading With Help
For children who recognize some words and sound out others with help
• short sentences • pattern stories • simple plotlines

Reading On Your Own
For children who are ready to read easy stories by themselves
• longer sentences • more complex plotlines • easy dialogue

First Chapter Books
For children who want to take the plunge into chapter books
• bite-size chapters • short paragraphs • full-color art

Chapter Books
For children who are comfortable reading independently
• longer chapters • occasional black-and-white illustrations

There's no need to hurry through the Miles. Road to Reading is designed without age or grade levels. Children can progress at their own speed, developing confidence and pride in their reading ability no matter what their age or grade.

So sit back and enjoy the ride—every Mile of the way!

Library of Congress Cataloging-in-Publication Data
Mayer, Mercer.
Little Critter sleeps over / Mercer Mayer.
    p.   cm. -- (Road to reading.   Mile 2)
Summary: Little Critter goes to visit a friend where someone in
funny clothes opens the door, the napkins are folded to look like
hats, and the bedroom is very dark.
ISBN 0-307-26203-0 (pbk.)
[1. Sleepovers--Fiction.]   I. Title.   II. Series.
PZ7.M462Lb   1999
  [E]--dc21   97-80729
                                                                                    CIP
                                                                                    AC

A GOLDEN BOOK • New York
Golden Books Publishing Company, Inc. New York, New York 10106

ISBN: 0-307-26203-0   A MCMXCIX

LITTLE CRITTER®
SLEEPS OVER

*To Arden,
the New Little Mayer*

BY
MERCER MAYER

I am going to sleep over
at my friend's house.

His house is big.

Someone in funny clothes
opens the door.
I see my friend.

I say good-bye
to Mom.

I say hello
to my friend's pool.

We splash.
We swim.
We paddle.
We float.

We hit the ball
over the net.

Sometimes we hit the ball
too hard.

We play hide and seek
for a long, long time.

13

Then we go inside.
My friend has all of the
Bozo Builder set.

He has a train
that can loop around
and go fast.

His bear is big—
bigger than my bear.

But his dog
is small.
His dog is named
Froo-Froo.

It is time for dinner.
The napkin looks
like a hat.
I put it
on my head.

After dinner
we watch TV.
My friend has a TV
in his room.

It is time for bed.

We turn out the light.
It is dark—
darker than my room.

I pretend that
I am at home.
I hug my bear.

The next day
we play with the hose.
Froo-Froo likes
the hose, too.

No, Froo-Froo!
Come back!

We run.

We dive.

We jump.

We climb.

Got you!

It is time to go home.

I call Mom.

I say good-bye
to my friend.

Thank you
for everything.

Sleepovers
are fun.
But home is best.